The TRANSFORMERS™— Robots in Disguise!

They came from Cybertron—a planet of machines—where war raged for thousands of years between the noble Autobots and the evil Decepticons.

NOW THE BATTLE OF THESE POWERFUL ROBOTS IS YOUR BATTLE!

ONLY YOU can protect the earth from the evil destruction of the Decepticons!

Read the directions at the bottom of each page. Then decide what the Autobots should do next.

If you decide correctly, the Autobots will triumph! If you make the wrong choices, the unspeakable evil of the Decepticons will rule the world!

Hurry! The adventure begins on page 1.

THE TRANSFORMERS™

Battle Drive

by Barbara and Scott Siegel

BALLANTINE BOOKS • NEW YORK

Library of Congress Catalog Card Number: 85-90607

ISBN: 0-345-32670-9

Editorial Services by Parachute Press, Inc.

Illustrated by William Schmidt

Designed by Gene Siegel

Manufactured in the United States of America

First Edition: December 1985

10 9 8 7 6 5 4 3 2 1

Bumblebee, the smallest of the Autobots, has been sent on a scouting mission by Optimus Prime. The Autobots' enemies, the evil Decepticons, have been very quiet lately. Surely they must be planning something. But what? Bumblebee has been driving all over the countryside looking for signs of a Decepticon attack. All he has seen are miles and miles of rich, rolling farmland covered with wheat and corn.

There can't be any Decepticons around here, Bumblebee decides. This farm country is so peaceful.

Since there is no sign of the Decepticons, Bumblebee decides to head back to headquarters. Suddenly a battered old pickup truck comes tearing down the road! Bales of hay tumble out of the back and go flying onto the roadway. The truck is heading straight for Bumblebee! The truck driver turns the wheel sharply and goes around Bumblebee.

Then, a split second later, a station wagon comes racing up from behind the pickup truck, weaving like crazy around all the bales of hay in the road.

Turn to page 2.

1

"What's going on here?" Bumblebee asks himself, puzzled. And then the puzzle becomes even more confused as a tractor and one, no two, no *three* more cars come speeding down the road toward him! And as they race past him, Bumblebee can see the faces of the humans inside. They look terrified! The passengers keep turning and looking out their back windows. Something is following them! But what?

Bumblebee looks back from where they came... and that's when he knows that his scouting mission was not in vain. *It's the Decepticons!*

Turn to page 8.

The Autobots instantly shut down their motors so they can listen to the faint sound of rumbling in the air.

"Sounds like . . . like jet engines," Bumblebee says nervously.

They all scan the sky, searching in every direction for a possible Decepticon attack.

"I see them!" cries Prowl. "They're coming from the north!"

"No!" exclaims Jazz. "I've spotted them, and they're flying here from the south!"

"You're both wrong," insists Wheeljack. "I see them and they're on the western horizon, coming on fast!"

"No, no! They're attacking from the east!" shouts Hound. "I can see them plainly!"

"Silence!" orders Optimus Prime. "Don't you understand? They're coming from all four directions! We've been surrounded out in the open. We're *trapped*!"

. . . .

You're trapped too. You have to turn to page 63.

Swoop and Buster Witwicky soar through the air. The other three Autobots race down the road at top speed. Before long they reach the mountains—and spot trouble.

"There!" cries Buster from his vantage point on Swoop's back. "I can see the Decepticons! They're attacking a cave opening at the bottom of the mountain range. That must be where my father is!"

The Dinobot dives to the ground. "You get off now," he says.

Prowl roars up a moment later. "Swoop, you fly up ahead," he suggests. "Maybe you can distract the Decepticons while we try to reach Sparkplug in that cave. Go now. Do your best!"

His best will have to be awfully good or else the hopelessly outgunned Dinobot will be blasted out of the sky!

Turn to page 9.

The Autobots zoom down the road that runs alongside the river, racing for the bridge. In front of them, blocking their way, is Soundwave, backed up by Laserbeak, Buzzsaw, and Frenzy. And behind this first line of Decepticons are still more of the hated enemy, who are descending out of the sky.

"You shall not pass!" declares Soundwave.

"We'll see about that," Optimus Prime replies. And with that, he blows his horn in the cabin of the huge tractor trailer and heads full tilt at the Decepticon roadblock.

Soundwave aims his concussion blaster gun at the front of Optimus Prime's engine and fires!

It has no effect!

Turn to page 69.

Prowl's wire-guide incendiary missile explodes against the chest of Megatron. But the powerful leader of the Decepticons just laughs! And then Megatron fires his fusion cannon and blasts Prowl's left leg to pieces!

Hound doesn't wait a second longer. He shoots his turret gun at Thundercracker and knocks the big Decepticon over onto his back. Meanwhile, Bumblebee uses Hound's covering fire to pull the wounded Prowl back to the cave.

Sparkplug Witwicky comes to Prowl's aid and uses his incredible knowledge of machines to get the damaged Autobot's leg back in working order.

The battle continues to rage for two full days. Sparkplug does everything that's humanly possible to repair the Autobots as they constantly get zapped by the powerful Decepticon forces.

Finally, though, Sparkplug can do no more. Prowl, Hound, and Bumblebee are creaking and squeaking—half of their parts no longer work.... But then, suddenly, Sparkplug sees a flash of light from the back of the cave. Could it be that there's actually a way out of this death trap?

If you think they can escape from the cave, turn to page 64.

If you still think Swoop will bring help, turn to page 50.

7

Bumblebee spots two of the most powerful Decepticons, Blitzwing and Starscream. They're attacking the farms! They are setting all the fields on fire. The big silos full of grain, the barns full of machinery—everything is being shattered by the Decepticons' attack. And now they're sweeping farther down the road, getting closer and closer to him!

What should the little Autobot do? Should he turn himself into his robot form and try to fight these Decepticons alone? Or should he hide by pretending to be a damaged vehicle on the side of the road?

If you think Bumblebee should stand and fight, turn to page 18.

If you think Bumblebee should pretend to be a damaged car, turn to page 22.

Swoop takes off to face the Decepticons. Up ahead is the mighty Megatron, as well as Laserbeak, a patched-up Blitzwing, Starscream, Bombshell, and at least half a dozen other deadly Decepticons.

They're moving in on the cave. Swoop must go into action quickly. The only advantage he has is that all their attention is centered on the cave opening. They're not looking up. And that's where Swoop is. Just like his name, the Dinobot swoops down at 250 miles per hour, heading right for Starscream.

With air-to-air missile launchers under each of his wings, Swoop is well armed. He dives right into the enemy jets! When he's practically right on top of the startled Starscream, Swoop lets go one of his missiles.

The impact is, well, explosive!

The missile has the power of five thousand tons of TNT! It sends Starscream crashing into the side of a mountain!

Turn to page 10.

But Swoop has no time to enjoy his victory! Every single Decepticon jet has turned to attack him! He's done the job he set out to do, distracting the enemy from the cave where Sparkplug is hiding. But now he's in trouble, and he's got to decide what to do next! Stand and fight? Or should he try to get away while he can?

The Decepticons are aiming right at him! He's got three seconds to make up his mind. One, two...

If you think Swoop should stay and fight, turn to page 25.

If you think Swoop should run and fight another day, turn to page 20.

Bumblebee has discovered the vicious Decepticon plan! As soon as Blitzwing and Starscream take off, he immediately rushes back to headquarters.

When he arrives, Jazz greets him with a worried look. "What happened to your roof?" he asks. "It looks as if a boulder hit you."

"No time to explain," Bumblebee replies as he rushes by. "I've got to find Optimus Prime!"

Jazz can see that the little Autobot is really worried. He follows Bumblebee into the big meeting room. And when he and the rest of the Autobots finally hear Bumblebee's report to Optimus Prime, all of them are shocked!

"They would actually try to starve the humans to death?" asks Hound.

"That's what they said," replies Bumblebee.

"These earth people have been good to us," announces Optimus Prime. "It's our duty as peace-loving Autobots to save the humans. We must leave at once and stop this evil Decepticon plot. I want five volunteers to go with me on this mission. Who wishes to join me?"

Turn to page 15.

Jazz can't stand it. "I'm going back to help Optimus Prime!" he shouts to the others. "Get to the bridge and hold it until we come back...*if we come back!*"

Veering on two wheels, Jazz makes a sharp turn and races back to help his friend. When he gets close, he changes into his robot form and fires his photon rifle at Soundwave, sending the sneaky Decepticon tumbling over backward. Then he uses his flamethrower to scorch the Insecticon, Bombshell. Now there are just eight Decepticons swarming over Optimus Prime—and soon there are just seven when Optimus Prime fires his laser rifle at Starscream.

The Decepticons pull back in fear. That's all the time Optimus Prime needs. He looks back and sees that the other Autobots have fought their way to the bridge. "Jazz, you disobeyed my direct order!" he calls out. And then he smiles and adds, "Thanks."

"Anytime," Jazz replies with sincerity.

"Let's get out of here while we still have a chance," says Optimus Prime. "Come on!"

Will they make it to the bridge before the Decepticons attack again? Turn to page 45.

12

"Did you destroy all the farmland in your sector?" demands Megatron, the powerful leader of the Decepticons.

"Yes, Megatron," replies Starscream. "Everything here is in total ruin."

"Very good. Soon the entire earth will be in our hands. Once we control all the food on the planet, the humans will have no choice. They will have to do our bidding—or they will starve!"

Bumblebee can almost feel his gas line freeze up when he hears Megatron's chilling words. Now he knows what the Decepticons are planning. Now his only mission is to get to Optimus Prime. He and the rest of the Autobots must save the human race from starvation or slavery—or both!

Turn to page 62.

14

The meeting hall is filled with cries of "I'll go!" "Me! Choose me!" "I want to go!" "I volunteer!"

Optimus Prime is touched by their devotion. None of them would miss the chance to fight alongside him. "I thank you all," he says.

"But our headquarters must remain protected at all times. Of all of you who have bravely volunteered to fight the Decepticons in the cause of the earthlings, I will choose Jazz, Prowl, Hound, Wheeljack, and Swoop."

"What about me?" demands Bumblebee.

"You've done your job—and you performed well. I can ask no more of you, my brave little friend."

"But I want to go!" insists Bumblebee. "Blitzwing banged up my roof and I want to be there when we teach him a lesson!"

Optimus Prime smiles. "So be it. You shall join us also. And now, let us begin our journey. For tomorrow we shall drive into battle!"

Turn to page 27.

Jazz wants to go back and help Optimus Prime, but he knows his duty is to stick with the rest of the Autobots. But he makes the right decision because, thanks to Optimus Prime single-handedly holding back three quarters of the Decepticon army, the six of them—Jazz, Hound, Wheeljack, Prowl, Swoop, and Bumblebee—manage to fight their way to the bridge.

Optimus Prime soon follows after them.

Just as they're all crossing over the bridge, though, a blast from Megatron's nuclear-charged fusion cannon vaporizes the far end of the structure!

The bridge, with all the Autobots on it, collapses into the raging river below.

Hold your breath and turn to page 59!

"Follow after me as fast as you can!" Optimus Prime shouts at Jazz. And then the leader of the Autobots rumbles toward a showdown with the Decepticons who are pushing Hound, Prowl, Wheeljack, Swoop, and Bumblebee off the bridge.

He joins the fight at the foot of the bridge without a second to spare. His fellow Autobots are damaged and their circuits are on overload. *Even worse—the Decepticons are trying to blow the bridge apart!*

If the bridge is destroyed, Optimus Prime and Jazz will never get across the river. They'll be cut off ... and then cut down!

Using every bit of power at his command, the leader of the Autobots smashes through the Decepticons and then stands like a giant with his laser rifle outstretched, firing at every single Decepticon he can get a bead on. In the meantime, Jazz races toward the bridge, with Megatron trying to turn the speeding Autobot into molten metal with his nuclear-charged fusion cannon.

Jazz is getting closer but Optimus Prime and the others can't hold the Decepticons off much longer. "Hurry!" Optimus Prime yells at Jazz. "Hurry!"

You had better hurry, too, and turn to page 66!

17

He may be small, but Bumblebee has the same courage that runs through the fuel lines of all the great Autobots! And with the element of surprise on his side, he figures he just might have a chance!

As Blitzwing and Starscream get closer, Bumblebee readies himself for a quick transformation into his robot form. If he can quickly knock one of the enemy out of the sky, then the odds won't be so heavily against him anymore. But that will depend on perfect timing. And that means he can't afford to miss!

The Decepticons are zooming toward him at supersonic speed. They're flying low to the ground, destroying everything in front of them. It's only a matter of seconds before they reach him. When they're two thousand yards away, Bumblebee fights back the urge to jump into action. They're still too far away.

At one thousand yards his engine starts to rev up in anticipation...but he still holds back.

In the blink of an eye the Decepticons are only five hundred yards away. Then four hundred, three hundred, two hundred, one hundred...

Hurry! Turn to page 30!

Swoop decides to make a run for it, hoping to draw as many Decepticons as possible into chasing him. If they come after him, then Buster and the others will have a better chance of safely reaching Sparkplug in the cave.

At a blazing 250 miles per hour, Swoop turns and heads for home...and at least half a dozen Decepticons chase after him.

It works!

Swoop looks over his shoulder and sees Prowl, Hound, Bumblebee, and Buster entering the cave. Now all he has to do is stay in one piece and get to Autobot headquarters.

Go on to page 21.

Meanwhile, Sparkplug and his son, Buster, hug each other as the three remaining Autobots prepare to fight the small army of Decepticons who still remain outside the cave.

Will Swoop make it back to headquarters in time to save the other Autobots?

"Maybe I should take Sparkplug and his plans to Optimus Prime," Prowl offers. "I am fast."

"No," Sparkplug says. "I don't want to leave Buster and Bumblebee here under attack."

"Dad, I think you should go," Buster says. "It will double our chances of survival."

What do you think?

Keep everyone together and hope Swoop brings help in time? Turn to page 34.

Let Prowl and Sparkplug try to reach Optimus Prime with the plans? Turn to page 41.

Bumblebee quickly pulls over to the side of the road and lets the air out of one of his tires. He opens the driver's side door to make it look as if the driver has left the car there. And then he sits and waits as the Decepticons draw near.

With fires turning the air into a choking, swirling haze of smoke, Blitzwing and Starscream stop their attack. They transform into their true Decepticon forms. They look over the damage they've caused with great pride. They walk over and stand right next to Bumblebee!

"The humans will be easy to destroy," Blitzwing says with confidence. "Once we've burned all their food, the planet will be ours!"

"You forget about the Autobots," Starscream reminds him.

"The Autobots?" Blitzwing laughs. "I don't fear those four-wheeled pieces of junk. If there was one right here I would pulverize it with just one fist." As if to make his point, Blitzwing brings his right fist down in a smashing blow to Bumblebee's roof.

The little Autobot has to hold in a groan of pain.

Go on to page 23.

"No," boasts Blitzwing, "the Autobots will give us no trouble."

"But before we fight the Autobots, we must finish the complete starvation of the human race. That is Megatron's order," Starscream says firmly.

"Then let's get on with it. The sooner we rid the planet of these troublesome humans, the happier I'll be."

Turn to page 11.

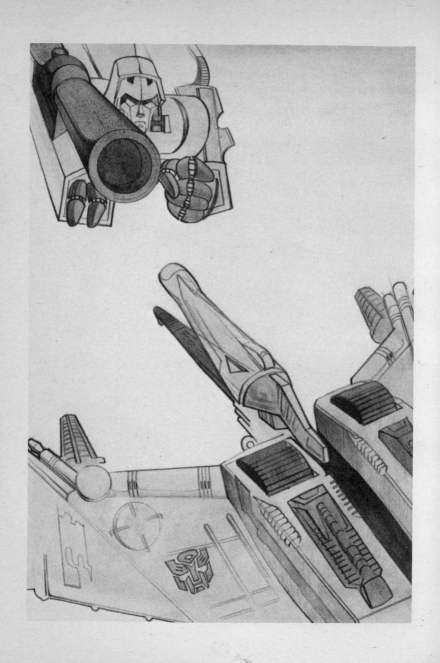

Swoop grunts in defiance as enemy fire fills the air all around him. Miraculously, nothing hits him. He seems untouchable!

Swoop sees Megatron at the center of all the Decepticons. "Kill the head and the body dies," Swoop has heard. So he dives right toward the leader of the Decepticons—and right into the sights of Megatron's fusion cannon!

Hurry! Turn to page 48!

Before they get back to headquarters, there's a terrible storm, with howling winds and sheets of rain. With the roads flooded and the bridges all washed out, traveling by car is totally impossible.

That leaves the Dinobot, Swoop, as the only possible way of getting news of the Decepticon plan back to Optimus Prime. But even Swoop can't fly in the swirling, one-hundred-mile-per-hour winds. Within just a few seconds he crashes to the ground.

It's hopeless. The Autobots are stranded in the middle of nowhere. And back in the middle of the lush farm country, where the weather is sunny, the Decepticons are burning acre after acre of grain, wheat and corn—the basic foods of human life. And there is no one to stop them!

Prowl was right. There wasn't enough time to get reinforcements. The choice you made doomed yourself and the rest of mankind to going to bed (forever) without dinner...or breakfast...or lunch...or ice cream...or cake...or cookies...or anything.

THE END

26

While the Autobots begin their long journey toward farm country, Blitzwing and Starscream are back at Decepticon headquarters. They are making their report to Megatron.

"And you're certain the Autobot spy believed your story?" asks Megatron.

"Absolutely," answers Blitzwing. "We fooled him completely. I have no doubt that the Autobots will try to stop our destruction of the crops, and—"

"And that," says Megatron with a smile, "will mean that we've drawn the Autobots into our trap! They'll be caught out in open, flat farmland where we can use our air power to blast them once and for all."

Now *you* know the truth...but how can you help the Autobots?

If you think you can pass the Autobots a warning message, turn to page 32.

If you think Optimus Prime and the Autobots can take care of themselves—quick, turn to page 42 and find out!

Yes, it's as bad as it seems. In fact, it's worse! The Autobots get creamed! Have you ever had Cream of Autobot?

No?

Well, you start by making a choice that puts Optimus Prime and his friends in plenty of hot water. Add about a zillion Decepticons who want to grind the Autobots into a melted mess...then let the Autobots boil under all that Decepticon fire power— and there you have it: Cream of Autobot. It doesn't taste very good, but then, defeat always leaves a bitter taste in the mouth.

Maybe next time you'll make the choices that lead to the sweet taste of victory.

THE END

The decision is made. The three Autobots—Bumblebee, Hound, and Prowl—and the Dinobot, Swoop, will try and stop the full might of the Decepticons.

Their plan is to try and convince the Decepticons that the entire Autobot army is attacking! Maybe they can fool them into a retreat.

It seems like a good plan. But what they don't know is that lurking nearby is the sneaky Decepticon spy, Soundwave. He hears everything!

While the Autobots head down the road to confront their enemy, Soundwave reports their plans directly to Megatron!

Turn to page 37.

As Blitzwing flies right over Bumblebee's rooftop, the tiny Autobot transforms! He turns himself into his true Autobot shape—which is twice as tall as when he's a car. With his fists raised high over his head, Bumblebee slams his whole arm into the underside of Blitzwing. The Decepticon jet spins into a shattering crash landing!

When Starscream sees Blitzwing go down, he figures that he's under a heavy Autobot attack. He radios for help, and then turns to face the Autobots! He's sure he'll see a full army of Autobots led by Optimus Prime. But all he sees is a single, small Autobot—Bumblebee.

"What a fool," Starscream says to himself with a laugh. "I'll blow that tiny hunk of junk into a million pieces!"

Roaring toward the nearly defenseless Autobot, Starscream shoots a deadly load of cluster bombs. But Bumblebee quickly dives behind the hay that has fallen out of the pickup truck. The impact of the explosion is absorbed by the bales.

Turn to page 67.

Use anything you've got handy—a pencil, a pen, a crayon, a felt-tip marker—and write your warning right here on this page. If you're lucky, Optimus Prime and the other Autobots will pass this way and see it before they're caught in the Decepticon trap.

When you're finished writing, turn to page 35—and find out if they will find your message.

Optimus Prime has decided to keep his forces together!

"See that bridge in the distance?" he asks.

The others all nod their heads.

"That's where we're going. If any Decepticons get in our way, we blast 'em!"

"That will take care of the Decepticons in front of us," Jazz says, "but what about the ones on the other three sides? They'll have a clear shot at our backs—which is just what the Decepticons would like! Shouldn't some of us stay behind to hold the enemy off?"

"You may be right," Optimus admits, "but I don't want to leave any of you behind to face certain destruction. Either we all make it out of here together, or we don't make it at all. Are you ready?"

"We're ready," says Jazz. "You know we will follow you anywhere."

"All right, then, let's take that bridge!"

If you don't want to get left behind, you'd better turn to page 5.

The Autobots decide to stick together and wait for Swoop to bring help. But how long will it be until Swoop returns? It could be days. It could be never. But the Autobots can't think about the future. All that matters now is the present....

A blast from Megatron's nuclear-charged fusion cannon reminds them of their peril. The shock of the blast above the cave causes an avalanche. Tons of rocks and boulders come roaring down the mountain, and the entrance to the cave is sealed off! Sparkplug and Buster, as well as all the Autobots, have been buried alive!

Hold your breath and turn to page 39!

As the small force of Autobots races deeper into farm country, Jazz suddenly slams on his brakes and starts to turn around.

"What is it?" asks Optimus Prime. "Why are you stopping?"

"I thought I saw some kind of message back there," Jazz replies cautiously.

"A message? You mean for us?" Bumblebee asks.

"That's what it looked like. I'm gonna go back and check it out."

"No, you're not," announces Optimus Prime. "It's probably a Decepticon ambush. Let's go—we're moving on!"

It isn't long before they find that the Decepticon ambush isn't back behind them—it's right in front of them. When the Autobots turn around the next bend, they drive over a road full of nails! Every single tire goes flat! Unable to move, the Autobots watch in horror as Decepticons storm out of the surrounding wheatfields.

If only the Autobots had read your warning!

Now they aren't going to read anything ever again, because the Decepticons have "nailed" them!

THE END

As this small group of Autobots heads deep into the heart of the richest farmland in the country, they're constantly on the lookout for the main force of Decepticons. They're sure that a big battle could be around the very next turn. But it isn't a battle they find when they come barreling around a corner.... It's Buster Witwicky, lying dazed in the road!

Quickly they revive the boy. As he opens his eyes and sees the Autobots, he cries out, "They're after Sparkplug! You've got to help him!"

Turn to page 71.

Bumblebee turns to look at his fellow Autobots. This is important information. But right now they're on a vital mission. Each of them is wondering what they should do....

"You've got to help Sparkplug!" young Buster implores them. "There is a Decepticon patrol after him! Every minute counts. Please! If you save him and get his blueprints of the Decepticon circuitry, we could defeat the Decepticons once and for all!"

This is a difficult decision to make. If the Autobots go after Sparkplug Witwicky, it means the Decepticons may be able to destroy all the food! But if Sparkplug has really found a way to defeat the Decepticons, then maybe the risk is worth it! The fate of the world depends on this decision!

....

If you think the Autobots should stick to the original plan to stop the Decepticons from destroying the world's food supply, turn to page 49.

If you think the Autobots should go after Sparkplug Witwicky instead, turn to page 51.

38

All is not lost....

Prowl saves the day by firing his high-corrosive acid pellets at the cave mouth, and they dissolve all the rocks that block the opening.

"Good job!" exclaims Hound. "Now let's bring the fight to them!"

"Yeah!" shouts Bumblebee. "The best defense is a good offense. Let's go get 'em!"

Turn to page 70.

"What I have here," Sparkplug says with enthusiasm as he reaches for his back pocket, "is just what you Autobots need to finally defeat the Decepticons. It will wipe out—"

Sparkplug suddenly becomes speechless. The blueprints of the Decepticon circuitry were destroyed in the battle! All he has in his hands are tattered pieces of paper covered with motor oil.

"Oh, no!" he cries. "I'll have to figure it out all over again!"

"And by then," Prowl says dejectedly, "the Decepticons will have changed their circuitry."

"Then this was a complete failure!" cries Bumblebee.

"No," announces Optimus Prime with a smile. "It was a victory. After all, the Decepticons don't know that Sparkplug's blueprints were destroyed. They'll be in hiding until they've redesigned their circuitry. Until then there will be peace on the planet earth. That, my friends, is victory enough!"

THE END

"Okay, I'll go," says Sparkplug.

"Are you ready to ride?" asks Prowl.

"As ready as I'm gonna get," replies the human as he snaps on his seat belt.

"Okay, you guys," says Hound, "you'd better get going. Me, Bumblebee, and Buster will hold off the Decepticons for as long as we can, but don't count on much of a head start. Make every second count... and good luck!"

Prowl just grins. There's nothing he likes better than a good race. But this is one race *he has to win!*

The speedy Autobot takes a deep breath, pulls up to the mouth of the cave, and gets ready to burn rubber.

The Decepticons are waiting....

Turn to page 46.

As the small team of Autobots begins its journey into the farmland's wide open spaces, Optimus Prime begins to wonder if he's making a mistake. But then he remembers that without help, the humans will be completely wiped out. So he forces the doubts out of his mind and continues on toward his fate.

Turn to page 57.

Bumblebee quickly transforms into his car form. His tires screech as he races for the safety of the burning cornfields. Perhaps he'll be able to hide in the tall cornstalks.

Bumblebee makes it across the road! He's just about to enter the cornfield. It looks as if he's going to make it! Then Starscream's null-ray stuns him, disrupting his electrical system. . . .

He comes to a dead stop!

Desperately, Bumblebee tries to start his engine. Just as it finally comes to life, Bombshell's "stinger" punctures all four of the little Autobot's tires.

Poor Bumblebee. He's gone as far as he's going to get on this scouting mission. He won't discover the reason behind the Decepticon attack this time. In fact, you might say he's all "tired" out. And his adventure is at an

END

"All of you," Optimus Prime calls out in his commanding voice, "fight your way to that bridge. I'll stay here and hold the rest of the Decepticons off. Hurry, now . . . and good luck!"

"But what about you?" Jazz cries. "You can't stay here alone!"

"Do as I say!" orders the brave Autobot leader. "I want all of you to be safe."

Jazz and all the other Autobots begin to race toward the bridge. But Jazz can't help but look back through his rearview mirror. What he sees makes his radiator boil up with anger: Optimus Prime is being attacked by no less than *ten* Decepticons!

If you think Jazz should disobey orders and go back to help his leader, turn to page 12.

If you think Jazz should do as Optimus Prime ordered and head for the bridge, turn to page 16.

"Don't let them get away!" Megatron orders.

The Decepticons rush after the two fleeing Autobots, coming at them from behind. In no time at all they can see the red taillights of Optimus Prime and Jazz.

The Decepticons like nothing better than to strike from behind—it's just their style.

Laserbeak smiles as he fires his laser cannon at Jazz's left rear tire. The blast misses Jazz, but the force of the explosion next to the wheel sends Jazz into a terrible spin!

Turn to page 68.

As soon as Prowl roars out of the cave, Hound has a great idea. He uses his hologram gun to project the illusion of *three* Autobots who look just like Prowl. The three phony Autobots screech off in *three* different directions!

The Decepticons don't know which is the real Prowl. They don't know which Autobot to shoot at or which one to follow!

But Hound doesn't have that problem. He knows whom to shoot at! He blasts a wing off the vicious Insecticon, Bombshell.

Bumblebee and Buster push a huge boulder off the edge of the cliff. It crashes down onto Megatron. It nearly knocks him over!

Unfortunately, Hound's hologram gun can only create an illusion for a very short time. The extra two images of Prowl suddenly disappear, and there, in the distance, Laserbeak and Blitzwing spot the dust cloud of the real Autobot! They immediately take off in hot pursuit!

Turn to page 54.

46

Swoop can see that he's looking right down the barrel of Dinobot death. He's got to be the one to fire his weapon first or Megatron will vaporize him. And with only one missile left he's got to make that single shot count. . . .

Swoop fires, aiming his missile right at Megatron's head. But just then the huge Decepticon leader steps forward and raises his own weapon. At the very moment Megatron fires, Swoop's missile whistles right down the bore of the Decepticon leader's gun . . . and the explosion blasts the once-towering Megatron in half! Swoop cuts him down to size—literally!

The rest of the Decepticons are so stunned that Swoop manages to get away without being attacked. Still, the Decepticons figure they can destroy the others that Swoop left behind. But it isn't long before the Dinobot roars back with Optimus Prime and the rest of the Autobots. He brought help! And without Megatron to help the Decepticons, it's an easy Autobot victory! Swoop did it! He's a hero!

The only bad part is that you've run out of story. But you can open the book again whenever you're all "revved" up and ready for the action of *Battle Drive*!

THE END

Trying to save the world from starvation is a noble idea. Too bad Megatron doesn't agree. And he knows (thanks to Soundwave) that the Autobots are coming. . . .

The four brave Autobots don't make it very far. A huge force of Decepticons comes hurtling out of the sky from every direction.

The battle is ferocious—but very one-sided. The clash of the Transformers lasts just a few minutes. When it's over, only the burning hulks of four brave machines are left.

There's really nothing more to say now. It's just a case of "Ashes to ashes and rust to rust. . . ."

THE END

The battered Autobots barely have the strength to lift their weapons. They counted on Swoop but he hasn't come back. And now they can hear Megatron and the other Decepticons laughing as they approach for the kill.

But suddenly the laughing stops! There's the sound of explosions! Buster Witwicky crawls to the edge of the cave, looks out, and cries, "Swoop is back! He's got Optimus Prime and a whole army of Autobots!"

Optimus Prime rams through the Decepticon defenses. Behind him roars a fleet of Autobots! The sun reflects brightly off their chrome. And when they transform themselves into their true Autobot shapes, the firepower they unleash is awesome!

Windcharger, Tracks, Powerglide, and Topspin come right up behind Optimus Prime and begin blasting away at the startled Decepticons.

Turn to page 58.

"We've got to save Sparkplug," Bumblebee says. The others agree.

"Which way did he go?" asks Bumblebee.

"He headed that way!" Buster says, pointing toward the mountains in the distance. "He figured that if he could get off this open land and into the hills, he might be able to hide." Sparkplug's son looks pale. "But I don't think he can get that far . . . not with the Decepticons so close behind him."

"Well," Hound offers, putting one of his big mechanical arms around the boy, "your father is a pretty resourceful fellow. I'm sure he'll be just fine. And when we catch up to those Decepticons, we'll teach them a thing or two. Right, Autobots?"

"Right!" they all shout together.

"Can I come with you?" asks Buster. "I'll help any way I can."

"It's going to be dangerous," warns Bumblebee.

"I'm not afraid of those Decepticons—not if I'm with you guys!"

The four of them look at each other, and then they all nod their heads. They like this spunky kid.

Turn to page 52.

"Climb on back," grunts Swoop. "I give ride!"

As soon as Buster is settled up on the Dinobot's back, Prowl shouts, "Let's get going!" And with that, they all roar down the road, heading straight for the mountains—and a battle with the Decepticons!

Turn to page 4.

Prowl is fast, but he's no match for these jet-powered Decepticons—and he knows it. What Prowl has going for him, however, is his ability to make quick turns and sudden stops. He hopes this will keep him from ending up in a scrap-metal yard.

"Hold on!" Prowl yells at Sparkplug. "This is when the ride *really* gets bumpy!"

Just as Laserbeak and Blitzwing dive at the fast-moving Autobot, Prowl swerves off the road. Then he jumps over a ditch and drives straight toward a forest.

"You'll never be able to maneuver through all those trees!" warns Sparkplug.

"I can maneuver through anything," Prowl replies.

The two Decepticons dive once more at their prey. But Prowl makes it to the trees. Then he keeps on going—madly turning left, then right, then right again, zigzagging around trees and boulders.

Suddenly there is a terrible *crash*!

Did Prowl smash into a tree? Did the Decepticons find a way to attack him despite the cover of the forest?

You'll never know until you turn to page 56.

Optimus Prime keeps up a steady fire with his laser rifle to protect Jazz until the speedy Autobot can get himself turned around and headed in the right direction. Those precious seconds almost spell the difference between success and failure. By the time the Autobot leader and Jazz reach the bridge, it's nearly too late. The Decepticons have pounced on Prowl, Hound, Wheeljack, Swoop, and Bumblebee. They're about to be wiped out...but Optimus Prime and Jazz arrive just in time to burst through the enemy forces and save their friends!

The battle for the bridge is ferocious. But the Autobots won't give up. They fight for every yard, every foot, and every inch. And finally they shatter the last defense of the Decepticons and roar over the bridge to safety!

Megatron's plan was a failure! The Autobots survive to fight another day...and that day will come when you have the courage to once again open this book.

THE END

That crash you heard wasn't made by Prowl or the Decepticon attack. It was made by *you,* falling out of bed! You must have drifted off to sleep while you were reading....

But if this is all a dream, what are you doing in this book, wearing your pajamas?

THE END

The Autobots continue deeper and deeper into farm country. Soon they're in the middle of a huge flat plain. On three sides there is nothing but miles and miles of waving fields of wheat. On the fourth side they are blocked by a river. There's the faint outline of a bridge in the distance. And across the river, on the other side of that bridge, are some rocky hills.

"I don't like this," says Wheeljack, looking around. "Why haven't we come across any Decepticons trying to burn all these fields?"

"It has me worried too," admits Optimus Prime. "And I don't like being out in the open like this. We're sitting ducks for a large Decepticon force."

No sooner does Optimus Prime utter those fateful words than Jazz suddenly says, "I think I hear something...."

Turn to page 3.

The Decepticons don't know what hit them! Laserbeak gets it right in the beak! Shockwave gets the shock of his life! And Starscream does plenty of screaming!

"Look at that!" cries Sparkplug from the mouth of the cave. "It's like an old Western with the cavalry coming to our rescue!"

Megatron's warriors begin flying off in every direction. It's a rout!

Later, Optimus Prime beams with pride at the brave Prowl, Hound, and Bumblebee who stood up to the Decepticon attack. "You did well, fellow Autobots," he announces for all to hear. "You and our friend, Swoop, can be very proud of yourselves. You protected Sparkplug Witwicky and his son. And now, speaking of Sparkplug...let's see these important blueprints of the Decepticon circuitry!"

Turn to page 40.

The Decepticons think that they've won.

But they haven't.

The river is moving so fast that the Autobots don't sink! The swiftly moving current carries them out of danger. The Autobots survive to fight another day. Oh, sure, they're a little wet when they finally get out of the river—but in the end it's Megatron's plan that turned out to be soggy.

THE END

Bumblebee can't fight off Starscream and Bombshell. His chances are much better if he tries to make it to the town. He may not be as fast as some of the other Autobots, but he sure knows how to maneuver. And he needs every bit of skill he has to avoid Starscream's null-rays and Bombshell's bullets.

The road around him is being blasted to bits! But, so far, Bumblebee has not been hit! And then Bumblebee gets a really lucky break! A thick, heavy cloud of smoke from the burning farmland drifts in his direction. Hidden by the smokescreen, Bumblebee manages to escape to the town. He parks himself in the used-car lot as the smoke cloud blows farther up the road.

Starscream and Bombshell follow him to town. But the smoke gets in their way. When it clears, they don't notice Bumblebee among all the other cars in the lot.

When Starscream transforms himself into a robot, he's standing no more than fifteen feet away from Bumblebee! And that's when Megatron, the leader of the Decepticons, radios a message. Bumblebee can hear every word!

Turn to page 14.

As soon as the coast is clear, Bumblebee races toward Autobot headquarters. He hasn't traveled more than a few miles, though, before he runs into his friends Prowl, Hound, and the Dinobot, Swoop.

"You're a sight for sore headlights!" he exclaims.

"And so are you," replies Prowl. "We've been looking all over for you. You have been gone a long time. Optimus Prime was worried."

"Well, he has got something to worry about, but it isn't me." All three of them listen quietly. Their expressions quickly grow grim as they hear Bumblebee's news.

At the end of the little Autobot's report, Hound says, "There's no doubt about it. We've got to hurry back and make sure Optimus Prime hears this!"

Prowl shakes his head and says, "No, there isn't time! The Decepticons could destroy thousands of acres of food before we get to Optimus Prime! We have to stop the Decepticons now—right away—before it's too late!"

Which plan do you think makes the most sense?

....

If you agree with Hound and want to get Optimus Prime and the rest of the Autobots, turn to page 26.

If you agree with Prowl and want to take on the Decepticons with this small group, turn to page 29.

The Decepticons seem to fill the sky! There are only seven Autobots against a full enemy army. Optimus Prime knows that to merely survive would be a great victory! But escape seems impossible. Yet there has to be a way!

That's when Optimus Prime remembers the bridge that crosses the nearby river. If they can get across that bridge, the Autobots might be able to make it to the hills on the other side of the river. The hills would give them some protection.

But how are they going to do it?

....

If you think the Autobots should stay together and fight their way to the bridge as one unit, turn to page 33.

If you think the Autobots should divide their forces, turn to page 44.

"Hey! I think I've found a way out of here!" exclaims Sparkplug. "Follow me!"

Prowl, Hound, and Bumblebee use their last reserves of power to drive deeper into the cave. But the farther they travel, the darker it gets.

"I'm positive I saw a glint of light," Sparkplug insists.

And he's right. Far in the distance they can see a pinhole of light. "We're saved!" cries Bumblebee.

They rush toward the opening...but in their haste, they fail to see the deep shadow in front of them—and they race out over the edge of a deep pit!

They go sailing off into space—falling and falling. Long before they hit the bottom, they know it's...

THE END

Jazz zigs and zags, avoiding the blasts from Megatron's fusion cannon. But while the Autobot is taking evasive action, the bridge is still being struck by heavy fire from the rest of the Decepticons.

Yet Optimus Prime refuses to budge.

He'll stand tall right where he is until either Jazz is safely across the river or the bridge collapses beneath him. He owes Jazz that much for saving his life before...and he won't let his friend down!

Thundercracker dives at the bridge and Optimus Prime shoots him out of the sky.

Laserbeak comes soaring down at the bridge and Optimus Prime blasts him out of the sky too.

Then—finally—Jazz zooms up to the bridge and races right between Optimus Prime's legs and makes it all the way across the bridge.

Moments later the bridge breaks apart and falls into the river! But Optimus Prime and the others are now safely in the hills. Enraged, Megatron and the rest of the Decepticons continue to attack....

....

Turn to page 72.

As Starscream flies past, Bumblebee hurls a big bale of hay at the Decepticon. It is sucked up into one of Starscream's jet engines. And it jams it up!

The plane begins to lose power and sputter!

Bumblebee is thrilled! He's won ... or so it seems ... until the ground at his feet explodes!

Starscream's call for help brought out the evil Insecticon, Bombshell! And Bumblebee is in his firing range. Worse still, Starscream has managed to gain altitude and is attacking Bumblebee from the other direction! The little Autobot is caught in a crossfire. Fighting back now would be suicide!

He could make a run for it through the burning fields. Earlier in the day he had passed a small town. Maybe he could go there and try to hide out in the local used-car lot. Either way, his chances of survival are very slim! What should he do?

....

If you think Bumblebee should make a run for it through the cornfields, turn to page 43.

If you think Bumblebee should try to hide out in the used-car lot, turn to page 60.

67

Optimus Prime starts to slow down to help the stricken Autobot.

"No! Keep going!" Jazz cries. "I'm okay. I'll catch up to you," he promises.

Optimus Prime wants to help Jazz. He owes him that, but then he sees a force of Decepticons attacking the bridge. The other Autobots are desperately trying to hold the bridge rather than running to the safety of the hills beyond.

Should Optimus Prime stay with Jazz or help hold the bridge in the hope that Jazz will catch up? If the bridge is lost, then neither one of them will get away. What should he do?

If you think Optimus Prime should stay with Jazz, turn to page 55.

If you think Optimus Prime should go on ahead to help hold the bridge, turn to page 17.

68

Optimus Prime keeps right on coming and Soundwave is forced to jump out of the way. The rest of the Autobots follow right after their leader and keep racing for the bridge. But Laserbeak takes to the air and starts shooting his laser cannon at the road in front of the Autobots. He blows huge holes in the highway, making it impossible for Optimus Prime and the others to travel. The Autobots are at a dead stop ... with the emphasis on the word *dead*.

It looks bad for the Autobots. But is it as bad as it seems?

Turn to page 28 and find out.

Waiting outside the cave for them—in military formation—are more than half a dozen Decepticon warriors. On either side of the mighty Megatron stand Buzzsaw, Frenzy, and Ransack. On his other side stand Shockwave, Skywarp, and Thundercracker.

"Prepare to die!" bellows Megatron. "There will be no one left among you to shed your pathetic windshield-wiper tears. You are all going to be destroyed!"

"Talk, talk, talk," Prowl says sarcastically. "I bet your mouth is your biggest weapon!"

Megatron is furious! "You'll be the first to know my wrath!" he screams at Prowl.

"And you'll be the first to know mine!" replies the brave Autobot.

At the same instant they both fire their weapons!

Turn to page 7.

"What are you talking about, Buster?" asks Bumblebee. He has known the young boy since the Autobots first came to earth. "Who's after your father?"

"The Decepticons!" exclaims the boy. "I was trying to reach your headquarters to tell Optimus Prime when someone or something hit me from behind. You see, my dad's discovered what he thinks is a fatal flaw in the Decepticon circuitry. Only the Decepticons found out what he was doing, and now they're trying to catch Sparkplug before he can get his information to Optimus Prime."

Turn to page 38.

The hills make a natural fort. Using them for protection, the Autobots fight off wave after wave of Decepticon charges. Instead of an Autobot massacre, Megatron's plan turns into a Decepticon disaster!

A popular song—sung by all the Autobots—is born out of this battle. It celebrates the Autobot's incredible victory. It goes like this:

We went off to battle with Optimus Prime
And then were attacked by Decepticon slime.
Outnumbered and trapped, it looked like the end;
They tried hard to break us, but we wouldn't bend!
We discovered the truth by the time it grew dark:
The Decepticon bite is no worse than its bark.
The Autobot legend will surely survive—
It's all in a book we call *Battle Drive*!

THE END